The Freaky Joe Club

Illustrated by
John Manders

The Freaky Joe Club

Secret File #1:

The Mystery of the Swimming Gorilla

by

P. J. McMahon

ALADDIN PAPERBACKS
New York London Toronto Sydney

For The Condor, the real, true, and only one— P. J. M.

First Aladdin Paperbacks edition May 2004
Text copyright © 2004 by P. J. McMahon
Illustrations copyright © 2004 by John Manders

ALADDIN PAPERBACKS
An imprint of Simon & Schuster Children's Publishing Division
1230 Avenue of the Americas, New York, NY 10020

Designed by Lisa Vega
The text of this book was set in 14-point Minion.
Printed in the United States of America
10 9 8 7 6 5 4 3 2 1

Library of Congress Control Number 2003096178
ISBN 0-689-86260-1

Table of Contents

Chapter One

The Beginning

~~I lift my pen. I begin to write.~~ Nah.

~~It all began on a hot June day in Texas.~~ So big deal. It's always hot here in June.

~~The Condor sat waiting.~~ Nope.

~~Our tale mu~~st be told. All will be written down.

No, wait. That's okay.

I am The Condor. Well, anyway, that's my code name. Which must be used wisely. The rest of the time I am Conor. Not The Conor, just Conor. I am the founder of this Freaky Joe Club. And the Keeper of the Secret Files. This book will tell How We Began. Our Secret Stuff. All kinds of Important Things. So that one day, the world will know.

That is what Freaky Joe wants us to do.

I will write it as it happened, everything as I remember it on that first day:

The others are coming. I wait in The Secret Place. Which is an empty sort of Secret Place, but it's a start. I check our supplies: two beanbag chairs—one looks like a soccer ball, one like a baseball; a map of the United States and a map of the world, taped to the wall; extra tape to put them back up when they fall down, again; big sheets of paper; markers for writing on big sheets of paper; a bowl of bones and a bowl of water; we will need those bones.

CONOR

I have lined up a row of Useful Books for all-important fact checking and clue investigation. The books include:

a) MY favorite ATLAS OF THE WORLD with a yellow Post-it stuck on

the page for Madagascar. I am
interested in lemurs.

b) Three-volume set of ANIMALS OF
THE WORLD with a yellow Post-it
stuck in volume II to mark the
letter L.

c) GREAT BAD GUYS OF HISTORY. Very,
very useful. I bought it at the
library yard sale.

d) WORLD'S GREATEST DISASTERS.
Could help.

e) THE BIG BOOK OF UNDERSEA LIFE.
You never know.

f) An encyclopedia. Very old but still
has good stuff.

g) The complete series of Remington
Reedmarsh, Lemur Detective, in
case there is any spare time for
reading.

• • • •

There is another book, of course. Not just another book. The large red one, slightly chewed in one corner. It has a bicycle chain wrapped around it. A lock through the chain. Large words written on the front.

This is going to be great! is what I think.

Bang! is what I hear.

The door flies open, slamming the wall behind it. Leaving a hole in our new headquarters. My mother won't like that. I'll just have to tell her we're in a dangerous business.

"Am I first? I broke the land-speed record getting here." Jack bursts in. "What are we doing? Why did you tell me not to tell anyone?" Jack paces the room, his fingers snapping. Questions pop out of his mouth faster than I can answer them. "Who else is coming? When do we start?"

Jack does nothing slowly. He never sits still. He has to be first in everything. He competes about anything. He swears he breathes better than me.

He is my friend. And there will be only three.

"This is so cool." Jack flops on the soccer ball chair. "How did you get to use the studio?"

The Secret Place was, until yesterday, my mother's painting studio. She's an artist, and she worked here, in a room attached to the garage. With its own door.

"My mom wanted to swap this for the playroom. Because of the brushes," I explain, flopping into the baseball.

JACK

"Huh?" Jack asks, spinning the chair around and around. A beanbag chair, on a carpet floor. This is impressive.

"A friend sent her these special brushes from China. Big brushes." I show him.

"Do you get everything from China now?" Jack slaps his knee. The joke is not that funny.

"So she decided to paint big and wanted a

room with high ceilings. She's working on a painting the size of the wall."

Jack looks impressed. "How high?"

"She uses a ladder to get to the top." I'm not sure how high that is. "And I get to have this room, at least for the summer."

"What is she painting that's so big?"

"I dunno. It's green."

Jack gets to the important stuff. "Do we have to share this room with the Queen of China?"

"Jack, her name is still Bella." He means my five-year-old sister, who we adopted from China. Jack thinks she wants to rule the world. He just doesn't know how to handle her. "No, we don't have to share it with her." At least not for now. Things change.

"Do we get to bring the TV and GameBox out here?" he asks.

BELLA

"I dunno. Maybe. But it doesn't matter right now. We have more important things to do," I remind him.

"The GameBox always matters," Jack says in a solemn voice.

"Not as much as this club does. That is what Freaky Joe would tell you." I head toward the Red Book.

"What club? Freaky who? What's going on?" Jack is up, snapping, shouting rat-a-tat questions. Time to tell him. But then we hear it.

CRASH!

We hear "Ow!"

CRASH! Again.

"Ow!"

Silence.

"Dang!"

Jack stands still for one moment. He lifts his nose in the air like a lion sniffing for game.

"Timmy is here," he announces.

Chapter Two

Freaky Joe Underwear?

"Brilliant guess." I open the door before it can smash into the wall again. Timmy falls in.

"I crashed my bike," he announces.

"We heard." Before I close the door, I look outside. Slowly left. Then slowly right. From now on, we cannot be too careful.

There is nothing there. Only two bicycles, one red, one blue. Timmy's red one looks as if it's standing on its head.

"I landed on Jack's bike," Timmy admits. "So I'm okay. This is cool," he adds, "if a little empty. . . ."

"It's only the beginning," I explain.

"Well, it's a good thing I brought my own food." Timmy pulls a crushed package of . . .

something, uh, brown from his pants pocket. Something unknown and brown. He begins to eat it.

He is my friend. And there can be only three.

Timmy picks up a book. "Great. *Animals of the World*. I need an important question answered." Timmy sits, reading a brown book, eating brown food.

Jack steps over to look. "I read all three of those in one day."

TIMMY

"No, you didn't." I know Jack.

"No, I didn't. But I could have." Jack grabs Volumes II and III. Holding his arms out, he pumps *Animals of the World*.

"I think we should get started." I pick up the Red Book.

"If you know so much," Timmy asks Jack, "can you tell me if gorillas swim?"

"That depends on what country they're born in," Jack answers. "And aren't we supposed to be starting?"

Timmy slams the book, trapping brown food on the gorilla page. "So far they don't mention water. That could be important."

"This is important. Listen." I put on my best Giving a Report in Front of the Class voice. "The Freaky Joe Club starts today. And you can both be members. If you want."

Timmy stops eating for a moment. Thinking takes all his effort. "Okay. But who is Freaky Joe?"

Jack looks at him as if he is an idiot. "You don't know who Freaky Joe is?"

"You don't either, or you would have told me right away." Timmy only looks as though thinking is hard. He can do it. "And why does that book have a chain around it?"

I hold it up for them to see. On the cover in big black letters are the words:

THE SECRET FILES OF THE FREAKY JOE CLUB DO NOT OPEN IF YOU ARE NOT A MEMBER OR ELSE

"Or else what?" Timmy asks.

"Okay, who is Freaky Joe? Tell us quick!" Jack points two hands at me like he holds two six-shooters.

"I can't tell you. You aren't ready. First you have to prove yourselves as worthy members of the Freaky Joe Club. That's the way it's always done," I explain.

"So this is not the only Freaky Joe Club?" Timmy figures out.

"This is the only one around here now. There have been more. In other places, other times."

"This is good." Jack's snapping picks up.

"You can't join a Freaky Joe Club. You have to

be invited. There can be only three." I pause. This is important stuff. They both nod. Timmy raises three fingers.

"But how did you get invited? How come you get to start it? Tell me," Jack demands.

"I can't tell you that. But in time, all will be revealed." I practiced saying that before they came. It sounds as good now as when I did it in front of the mirror.

Timmy nods seriously.

I continue. "This room is now The Secret Place, headquarters of the Freaky Joe Club. If you agree to be members, you have to keep our secrets. You have to take a secret name. You have to learn our secret language."

"Okay, okay, and we have to wear special Freaky Joe underpants. We get it." Jack jumps up.

"No, there is no underwear." Though it might be a good idea.

Timmy stands. He raises his arm and salutes. "I promise. I want to join."

"I was just going to say that." Jack has actually come in second.

Timmy does an end-zone dance. "But I did first. Na na na boo boo."

"Na na na boo boo? Is that the secret language, or are you just an idiot?" Jack does his end-zone tackle. Nice move.

They slide across the empty room. Timmy almost loses his shorts, but gets off a nice kick to where Jack would wear his secret underwear.

I wait. They'll be done soon.

Jack sits up, his leg across Timmy's neck. "But why?"

"Why what?" Timmy asks. It's a little hard to hear him.

"Why have a Freaky Joe Club?" I guess.

"Yeah, what are we going to do?" The Timmy/Jack pretzel unwinds.

"What Freaky Joe wants us to do." I pause one minute. Okay, one second. "Solve crime. Fight evil."

"Yes!" Jack pumps his arm into the air. "I'll be great at that!"

"Is there anything else we have to do?" Timmy asks. His words are drowned out by a terrible noise.

"Oh, no," Jack cries.

A fearsome growl sounds through the air.

A banging noise.

A horrible howl.

"Yes," I answer Timmy. "You have to be brave."

I move away from the door just as The Beast bursts in.

Chapter Three

Not Just Any Name

The Great Black Beast runs into the room. Quick-thinking Jack grabs a bone. He throws it into a far corner, away from the Freaky Joe Club members. The Beast pauses. Stares at the bone. Stares at Jack. And runs hard at him, knocking him down. A full body block. The animal's mouth, exposing great sharp teeth, opens near Jack's exposed neck. Frozen to our spots, Timmy and I watch. And then—oh, no—the Great Beast leans over Jack. And begins, and begins . . . to lick his face.

"Get her off, get her off!" Lick. Lick. "Gross, get this dog off me." Big juicy lick. Jack pounds his hands and feet on the floor, looking like my little sister in full tantrum.

"Oh, come here, puppy," Timmy calls. My dog, Riley, leaps toward him. Timmy shares the brown food with her. Jack pulls his shirt up over his face, wiping hard. "You didn't say anything about Riley. What has Riley got to do with our club?" Jack rubs his face now with both sleeves.

RILEY

Hearing her name, Riley beats her tail in a drumroll. She munches food, looking happily at each of us in turn. Riley thinks Jack is wonderful. Jack doesn't like dogs.

"All Freaky Joe Clubs must have a Beast. This is a rule. From now on we must refer to Riley as The Beast. Which is her code name. She will be an important part of our crime-solving team." I look to each club member. "Is that okay?"

Timmy nods yes. Riley, assisted by Timmy, nods yes.

"The Beast is a good name for her," Jack answers, wiping his eyes with the hem of his shirt.

"She just wants to play with you. She likes you," Timmy the animal expert explains.

"She just wants to bite me and eat my flesh," Jack counters. "That's what Riley wants to do, don't you, Riley Girl?" Jack imitates Timmy talking sweet doggie talk. Riley thumps her tail some more.

"See, she's getting ready to attack. It's just like in those movies. People are hiding out, they hear drums, and they just know the bad guys are coming." Jack waves his arms, showing us how scared people act. Riley jumps up to help him.

"No, Riley!" Jack yells. He sets off running around the room. *Great fun*, thinks my dog. She chases. I catch her on their third circle around.

"Jack, stop fooling around. This is serious," I remind him. "This is the first meeting of the Freaky Joe Club."

"Fooling around? I'm lucky I'm alive." Jack starts finger snapping. "Okay, what do we do?"

"First, we have to decide on our secret names. We cannot do anything till we have our secret names," I explain.

"That way the bad guys won't know who we are?" Timmy gets it.

"You got it."

"But we'll still know who we are, right?" Jack paces, keeping a wary eye on The Beast.

"Yes, because we're the only ones who know each other's code names." This seems easy to me.

"And we know what you look like, Jack," Timmy reminds him. "You're the ugly one."

"But what if I don't look like me, because I'm in this great disguise, and we're having a really big fight, with lots of bad guys. You might not know what I look like." Jack pounds Timmy's head for effect.

"Then we call your code name, and you'll answer." I try again.

"Or we will figure, even in disguise, you are still the ugliest." Timmy is not being helpful. "So what are our code names?"

"Freaky Joe says every member should choose a code name. I am The Condor. Riley is The Beast. These names are written down in the book."

Timmy leaps up, his arms making muscles, his hands making fists. "I am Jimbo. I am ready to go!"

"Jimbo. I will enter your name in the book." I begin to unlock the chain.

Jack's turn. "And I'll be . . . I'll be . . ." His fingers snap to help his thinking. "I'll be The Jack!" he announces.

Timmy and I say at the same second, "The

Jack?" Even Riley tips her head to one side, a confused look on her face.

"What?" Jack asks, sticking his chin up high.

"Well, it's not much of a secret," I tell him.

"It's stupid," Timmy adds helpfully.

"You are The Condor, what's the diff?"

"A condor is something. He is the world's largest flying bird, a magnificent creature with a deadly beak that floats high above the world, seeing all, knowing all it sees." I have given some thought to my name.

"A Jack must be something."

"How about a small weasel from Madagascar that only eats dung beetles." I do not have three volumes of *Animals of the World* for nothing.

"Dung, Jack. So you want to be known as the guy who eats poop bugs?" Helpful Timmy again.

"Think of someone or something you really

like, that you admire," I suggest. "At least start there."

"I know—I will be The William Chase." Jack picks only the most famous hockey player in the world.

"Okay, so we want to be secret and not have people know who we are. Every time we say your name"—Timmy yells "Hey, William Chase" to demonstrate—"people are going to come running to get an autograph. Won't *that* be secret."

"It's not William Chase, it's The William Chase," Jack explains.

"Oh, that will fool them," Timmy answers.

"I like The William Chase," Jack insists. "Or The Jack." He crosses his arms. I can tell we're going to be stuck here for a while.

"Why don't you turn it around," I suggest. "We'll know who you mean, but no one else will. You could be Chase William, if you want."

"Yeah. Good. I like it. Chase William. Chase

William." Jack tries it again and again. Loudly. "Chase William. Chase. Chase."

The Beast knows that word. Maybe not that guy William, but she knows the other one.

"Chase. Chase." Finger snapping.

So The Beast does. Chase.

"No! Riley, no!" Jack starts to run.

"Stop running, Jack. She thinks you want to play." I grab for The Beast and miss.

"That's right, Riley," Timmy yells, "Chase William."

Jack throws open the door of The Secret Place and keeps running. Riley Chases William. The Condor and Jimbo chase Riley.

We catch up to them as Jack and The Beast are rolling around the side of The Secret Place. Where Jimbo's red bicycle stands on its head. All alone.

"Ah, Jack," Timmy asks as I sit on The Beast, "when did you move your bike?"

"I didn't move my bike. How could I move my bike? I was being attacked by a rabid monster." Jack sits picking grass out of his hair.

"You see, there was a blue bike here. And a red bike here. And now there's only a red bike here. Which means, take away one blue bike." Timmy does the math on his fingers.

Jack looks. Jumps. Yells. "My bicycle! My bicycle! Someone stole my bicycle!" He looks at Riley.

"She's a dog, Jack," Timmy explains. "And she has an alibi."

"Gentlemen," I announce, "the Freaky Joe Club has been formed. And now we have a crime to solve. Let's ride."

"Ride what?" Jack wails.

Chapter Four

For the Love of a Bicycle

"Do you think he'll stop soon?" Timmy questions.

Jack is running around and around yelling phrases such as "My bike!" and "My bicycle!" He points now and again to where his bike is not, looks at us, and says, "My bike?"

The Beast dances around with him, sure that the point of this game will shortly be revealed.

"He has to. Scientific studies have proven that a human being can only say the same word for a limited period of time." I watch Jack circling. "Or else they'll go mad."

"I say it's fifty/fifty which way he goes." When Riley gives up running for a minute, Timmy puts his arms around her neck. "Let's count the silly boy's words, hey, big girl? Oops. That's ten *bicycle*s."

"Keep your eye on him. I'd better tell my mom something's going on." I know that if I don't tell her, and later she hears about it, she'll be unhappy. The exact words she'll use will be: "Why didn't you tell me something was going on?"

"What do you think she'll do?" Timmy questions. "Fifteen *bicycle*s."

"I think she'll call the Big Guy," I admit.

"Oh, great." Timmy understands.

"I'd still better tell her." I head indoors.

"Did you hear that, Riley? The Big Guy is coming, yes, the Big Guy." Timmy holds Riley's collar as she tries to run away. "I know, I know, The Beast loves the Big Guy, but you'll have to wait. Nineteen, twenty."

The Condor flies from the scene. The first meeting of the Freaky Joe Club is not going exactly according to plan. But I was warned about that. Rule Number Twenty-Six B: Things Will Not Always Go According to Plan.

Well, Rule Number Twenty-Six B is true.

"Twenty-six *bicycles*," I hear Timmy announce.

I find my mother perched high on her ladder. She is drawing dark green circles in the upper corner of the canvas that covers one whole wall. They're good green circles. I explain the missing bicycle. I wait. She calls the Big Guy.

Which is why we're all standing here on my front lawn. The Condor, The Beast, Jimbo, a possibly deranged Chase William, and a Green Mother, all lined up. My mother is wearing mismatched, too-big clothing and a bandanna in her hair. She is mostly green. She holds one of the large Chinese brushes. My friends don't even notice. Even they are used to how odd she is.

"Mr. Butowski said he would be here in a moment," my mother explains. She waves her brush for emphasis. We nod our heads, keeping out of paint splatter range. "I'm sure he'll be able to straighten out this confusion. Are you sure you left your bicycle here, Jack?"

My mother intends to be helpful, I'm sure of that. She's a pretty nice person. As Timmy says, she likes kids and she's happy to feed them. This makes her perfect in his eyes. Nonetheless, she's an adult, and therefore asks useless questions.

Jack answers her. Sort of. "My bicycle," he moans.

"Thirty," Timmy counts.

"Pardon me?" my mother asks.

"My bicycle," Jack reminds her.

"I know, dear," my mother assures him. "I heard you."

"Thirty-one," Timmy answers.

"Pardon me?" my mother asks.

I can't take much more of this. Then I'm saved.

"Oh look, here comes the Big Guy!"

"That is Mr. Butowski to you." My mother is big on Respect for Grown-ups. Don't get her started on the kids on cereal commercials. That talk is longer than the wonderfulness of Chinese brushes.

"Yoo-hoo, Mr. Butowski, over here." My mother waves her brush in the air to get his attention. Because who would notice three boys, a dog, and a green parent standing in a row?

We all dodge the paint. Riley doesn't move quick enough. She is now The Beast with Green Spots.

Riley doesn't care about the paint. She sees the truck slowly coming up to our house. She knows who it is. She jumps, turns those happy dog circles, and says in doggie talk, "Oh boy oh boy oh boy."

Jack lands briefly on this planet. "You called the Big Guy?" he whispers.

"My mother did," I hiss back.

"Thanks for coming, Mr. Butowski," my mother calls happily. The purple truck comes to a halt. The purple truck with painted blue waves of water rolling from the front of the truck to the back. The purple, blue-waved truck with a lighthouse painted on each door. In the bright beacon of the lighthouse are the words SHIP'S COVE SECURITY. Just in case no one noticed the truck.

I seriously doubt that anyone would not notice the driver. Bubba Butowski, Ace Security Guard, unfolds himself from the front seat of the truck. Bubba is a Big Guy. There is no other way to say it. Well, there would be another word, but my mother wouldn't let me use it. But as these are the chronicles of the Freaky Joe Club, and it is important to be accurate and clear, I will say Bubba Butowski is a tall guy. And a Big Guy. If you see what I mean.

Bubba hitches up the pants of his uniform,

which has a lighthouse patch saying SHIP'S COVE
SECURITY SERVICE. He pushes back his white
straw cowboy hat with a wide brim saying SHIP'S
COVE SECURITY SERVICE. He sees, and addresses,
the most important being here.

Chapter Five

Big Bubba on the Job?

"Hey hey, big girl! Hey, Riley. The Big R. The Riley Girl. Who's a big baby? Who's a big girl? You are, yes you are, yes that's a good girl. The Big R. The Pooch. Do you need something to eat? Do you? Do you? Huh? Huh?" Bubba rubs, scratches, and hugs Riley.

Riley indicates that yes, oh yes, she is indeed hungry. "I'll be with you in a moment, Mrs. Moloney," Bubba says. "I think Riley needs a treat."

We all stand watching while Bubba extracts yet another dog biscuit from the bottomless well of dog treats that is the front seat of his truck.

"Mr. Butowski, the boys need to file a report. There has been some kind of problem."

"My bicycle," Jack says.

"His bicycle is missing," Timmy explains.

"Someone took my bicycle." Jack gets out a whole sentence. He comes back down to earth. His fingers snap. "Someone stole my bicycle." Yes! The Return of Jack.

"Maybe one of your friends borrowed it and forgot to tell you?" My mother is being an adult again.

"No one borrowed it. Someone stole it while we were having a meeting." Timmy eyes Riley's second biscuit. This could be the test of whether he will eat anything.

"Meeting of what?" Mr. Butowski wants to know.

"Just a meeting of friends," I quickly explain, glaring at Timmy, who clearly was thinking about gorillas when I mentioned the secret part of the club. "Friends gathered together for fun on a lovely summer day. No school, a little conversation, a little frivolity."

Maybe I'm overdoing it. Everyone, including Riley, is staring at me.

"But while we were talking, someone stole the bicycle." I nod my head up and down to show I'm telling the truth.

"I just know this is going to be some kind of misunderstanding," Bubba assures all of us. "We don't get that kind of stealing here in Ship's Cove." He smiles at my mother. "But I am on the job. And I'll write a report."

"Do you need me to sign anything?"

"No, ma'am, you go on back to your painting. I'll talk to the boys. I'm sure we're going to find one of their friends riding the bicycle." Bubba taps the side of his nose. "A Friend Who Makes Bad Decisions."

"I'll be upstairs if you need me, sweetie," my mother tells me. She waves good-bye with her paintbrush. Bubba retreats quickly to his truck. Riley sustains another hit.

But she snags another biscuit. And we get to listen to another accounting of Riley's wonderfulness.

"There you go," Bubba says. "Here's one for Riley. Can you shake? You can! What a big girl! Who's a smart girl? Who's a good girl?"

The Big Guy goes on and on. I quickly explain the truth to the members of the Freaky Joe Club.

"Tell him what he needs to know, and fast," I explain. "If we have any chance of solving this crime and retrieving the missing item," I can't bear to say the word, "we have to act now."

Jack looks confused, and about to name the missing object.

Timmy looks over at Bubba telling Riley what a good girl she is.

"It's too bad we couldn't convince him your bicycle is a dog," Timmy observes. "Maybe we should describe it as soft, brown, and fluffy."

Timmy has great potential to become Code

Name Jimbo the Detective. I knew he did. Which is why he was chosen.

For Bubba Butowski clearly believes that the key to neighborhood security is keeping all the dogs happy. The truth is: Bubba loves dogs. Which makes it hard not to like Bubba. No one loses a dog in this neighborhood. Bubba knows all their names. He has a long list of nicknames for each one. He knows their favorite treats and carries them. He sends them birthday cards. I think the dogs in our neighborhood run away from home just so Bubba can bring them back.

Bubba cannot stand to see a flower wilting. He stops to water them. He brings people their newspapers if it's raining or he knows they're sick. Mostly he takes care of the dogs. But solve crimes? Find bicycles? No, I don't think so. Not the Big Guy's specialty.

Bubba holds his clipboard, which has a pencil

dangling by a string. He licks the end of the pencil. Pauses to pet Riley. Hitches his pants again.

"Okay, what did you lose?"

Jack wails. We're about to lose him. Again.

"We didn't lose anything. Jack's bicycle was taken. Against his wishes. Stolen." In case I'm not being clear.

"From right here," Timmy adds.

"In Broad Daylight," I explain. "By a Nefarious Thief."

"Now that doesn't seem likely, does it?" Bubba scratches his head. Licks the pencil. "Tell me what it looks like. I'm sure I'll find it somewhere."

Jack begins. "It's blue. With green flames shooting down the side."

"Hold on a second, son," Bubba interrupts. "Can't you hear Riley barking? What is the matter, Big Girl? Are you hungry? Do you need a treat? Huh, is that what you're telling me? You are so smart." Bubba heads to his truck.

"Guys, we have to go *now*." I head toward the garage.

"Why?" Jack asks.

"Do you want to find your bike? Do you, do you? Huh, Big Jack? Who's a good boy?" I ask. "The Freaky Joe Club is your only chance."

Timmy understands. "Or do you want to take your chances with Bubba?" he asks.

Jack looks over where Bubba is rolling around on the ground with a biscuit in his teeth.

"Let's go," Jack agrees.

"On patrol," I declare. "I have a ride for you, Jack. But no complaining."

Jack looks at Mr. Butowski playing tug of war with Riley and the biscuit. Between their mouths. "I won't."

"We'll do this later, Mr. Butowski," Timmy calls.

"Okay, boys," the Big Guy calls. "Let me know how I can help."

Chapter Six

The Freaky Joe Club Rides

Freaky Joe's Rule Number Sixteen A: Be Thorough. Be Thorough. Be Completely Thorough.

Well, I guess Freaky Joe was clear about Rule Number Sixteen A. As we're at the start of our crime-fighting career, I intend to follow the instructions. We three will thoroughly, completely thoroughly check our neighborhood. From one end to the other.

"Goooo Slooower. I can't keep up," cries a voice from behind me. "Conor, where are we going?"

I stop my metallic green bicycle with the dragon head painted on the side fenders. Code

Name Jimbo rides up on his shiny red bicycle with special wheels. We turn to watch Jack wobbling down the street. On a bicycle that is no doubt too small. And no doubt too pink. But that is still, after all, a bicycle.

"Conor, you can't ride that fast if I'm going to be stuck riding . . . riding . . . riding . . . ," Jack splutters.

"Riding a Magical Baby Katie bicycle?" Timmy helps him out.

"Riding this," Jack answers.

"A cute little pink bicycle with sparkly streamers coming out of the handlebars? Oh, and a lovely white tail on the back fender? And let us not forget to mention the beautiful head of

Magical Baby Katie on the front of the handle-bars. A lovely unicorn's head with a darling unicorn's horn that lights up." Timmy is being helpful again.

"That's right, Timmy. Let's see if it makes as good a hat as it does a bicycle." Jack lifts the Magical Baby Katie bicycle up in the air. A bent bicycle will not make my mother or the Queen of China happy.

Most importantly, it will slow our patrol. Diplomatically, I step in.

"Are we going to solve crimes or act stupid?" I inquire. "Look, Jack, I'm sorry your bicycle was stolen. I'm sorry my sister wants to ride a bicycle that looks like a baby girl unicorn. She has that disease where everything she owns is pink or purple. And if you break the bicycle, Jack, you, and you alone, will explain it to her."

"Okay, okay, okay." Jack puts it down. Having to deal with my little sister scares him more than having to deal with my dog. He has no sisters. He has no defenses. If she cries, he'll give her anything he owns to make her stop. I do not have this problem.

"And I think those of us who have not had a bad thing happen should be nicer to those who have," I suggest.

"Okay, okay, okay. I was being a jerk," Timmy announces loudly. I hear him say softly, "You just inspire me, Jack." Jack doesn't hear; he is too busy making the unicorn's horn blink on and off.

"We have to start working together to solve the mystery," I remind them. "We have to start using our code names and acting like the detectives we are. You have to remember Rule Number Six: Always Remember What You Are Doing."

"How can we remember Rule Number Six if this is the first time we've heard it? And you didn't say anything about having to remember rules." Jack gets twitchy if he thinks anything involves homework.

"Can I read the rule book? I'll ride Magical Baby Katie if you let me read the rule book," Timmy promises.

"It is against the rules for you to read the rules until you have followed the rules. And one of the rules is to solve a crime. We're so lucky this has happened so early in our club," I assure them.

"So lucky." Jack seems unconvinced.

"So, The Condor, why are we at the boat?" Timmy gets into gear.

"Hey, maybe my bicycle is hidden in the boat. Great idea, Condor." Jack jumps up to investigate.

Our neighborhood, as anyone who sees Bubba's truck, or Bubba, will know, is called Ship's Cove. A brick wall surrounds the neighborhood, topped with life preservers that have been turned into lamps with nautical-type rope stretching between them. On a big wall at the entrance, the same rope spells out the words *Ship's Cove.* And in front of the wall is the back end of a boat.

An actual rowboat. Surrounded by flowers that, because of Bubba, never wilt. The flowers are planted to spell out *Ship's Cove,* just in case anyone has missed the idea that our neighborhood has a name.

It bothers me. What are we supposed to think about this rowboat? It looks like it dive-bombed to Earth. It occurs to me now that maybe it did. Maybe it's an alien lifeboat. And maybe, just maybe, Bubba is the commander of this alien lifeboat. This would explain a lot.

"You were wrong," Jack shouts. "My bicycle isn't hidden in the boat."

I do not point out that the boat is not big enough, or that I never suggested the bicycle was in the boat.

"My mistake," I admit. "Luckily this is a good place to start our patrol. We'll split up, carefully cover our routes, and meet at the pool."

"What do we do?" Code Name Jimbo asks.

"Look carefully at everything with new eyes. Detective eyes. Search for clues. Remember what you see, and we'll compile our notes," I explain. "Code Name Jimbo: You take Smooth Sailing Street and Ship's Cove Cove. Code Name Chase William: Take Safe Harbor Street and Land-lubber's Lane. All set? The Freaky Joe Patrol is on."

Code Name Jimbo jumps on his bike, saluting as he goes. "I'm on the job. See you at the pool."

At least I think that's what he says. He is eating, speaking, and peddling all at the same time.

Code Name Chase William rides off, wobbling as he goes. Magical Baby Katie's unicorn horn blinks on and off.

Chapter Seven

Water, Water Everywhere?

I take Ahoy Mate Boulevard, the main street. All's quiet on the Ship's Cove front. The Quinns' dog, Molly, barks and barks at me from behind her fence. After Riley, and Mrs. Bailey's Napoleon, Molly would be the dog voted most likely to be seen in Bubba's truck.

Miss Leona's very fat cat crosses the street slowly, pausing to roll over in the middle of the street. I remind myself to make a note that this cat may not be all she seems. Cats are supposed to be smart; that's what people say. Rolling around in the path of cars to scratch your back does not fit that description.

A truck passes. I memorize the words on the side. DOLPHIN POOL SERVICE.

I turn into Land Ho Lane. So does the Overnight Delivery Man, who drives too fast, as usual. My mom mixes it up with him. He rolls his eyes now when she flags him down. She always tells him she hopes someone somewhere is waiting on a kidney. Otherwise he is driving too fast.

Now he slows down in front of our house.

The security truck slowly comes at me the other way. Bubba yells "Hey" at me as he passes. Riley sits in the front seat munching. I would like to think The Beast is on the job. I know she is just cruising with her pal. Again.

I pass a truck with the sign LUCKY LARRY'S AT-HOME GROOMING SERVICE. YOUR PET. OUR SKILLS.

Freaky Joe should have suggested I rig up some way to write all this down while riding. I'm worried I might forget something that will turn out to be important. Lucky Larry is heading toward Smidgen's house. Smidgen is a teeny teeny tiny poodle with the goofiest haircut. And the best name. Great. Now I sound like I'm turning into Bubba.

I loop around into Crow's Nest Circle. The Special Squid Service for Pools truck comes the other way. A lot of people have pools here. Not just the fancy houses—any house. I guess it gets so hot here people just like seeing the water outside.

Water in your pool is the only water anyone is going to see in Ship's Cove. After we solve this mystery, I am going to try and find out why a neighborhood that is built on the Texas prairie is named for boats, water, coves, a shoreline, and all the stuff that is Not Here. Has Not Been Here and Then Dried Up. Will Never Be Here. There must be a reason other than the one my mother says: "There are foolish people everywhere you go, son. You just gotta roll with it."

I pass another one. Gorilla Pool Service.

And turn the corner by Mugsy's house. Who is my sister's best friend. Who is right now hanging upside down in a tree. With my sister.

"Hey, Conor," Mugsy calls.

"Hey, Mugsy. Hey hey, Bella," I answer.

"Hey hey, Conor," she answers. "We're hanging upside down to see which one of us gets sick first."

"Interesting game. Did Jack teach you that one?" Jack won't admit it, but he really likes my sister.

"No, it's Mikey's idea," Mugsy says.

MUGSY

Mikey is her younger brother.

"I think it's stupid," Bella says.

"I agree," I say. I decide to do the big brother thing. "You should probably get down before you get sick."

"But that wouldn't be as exciting," Mugsy says.

On that note, I head to the pool. Code Name Chase William is already there waiting. I am not surprised.

"I got here first," he declares. "Even though I had the slowest ride."

I am not surprised.

"But I saw a lot of good stuff," he insists.

Now I am surprised. I can hardly hear him over the noise from a game going on in the pool. Half the boys' swim team is in there.

Code Name Jimbo rides up fast. "I saw Bubba, and he had The Beast in the truck."

"I know. I'm sure The Beast is doing something useful," I lie.

And then, at that very moment, I see them. All of them.

"I saw four important clues," Code Name Jimbo announces.

"I saw five," Code Name Chase William snaps.

I count six of them. Holy Moly, this is bigger than we thought.

"Eight."

"Nine."

"Excuse me, The Condor?" Code Name Jimbo asks. "Are you hearing nothing we say? Do you not wish to break up this argument?"

There is a serious criminal at work around here.

"Condor, oh Condor," Code Name Chase William snaps his fingers in front of my face.

"His name is *The* Condor."

"The Condor, oh The Condor." Code Name Chase William snaps his fingers in front of my face.

"Look." I point.

"What?" Code Name Chase William wonders.

"Look there." I point.

"Bicycles in a bicycle rack," Code Name Jimbo explains.

"Exactly," I explain. "Now look in the pool."

Code Name Jimbo does. Code Name Chase William does. They look at the bikes.

"Oh, no." Code Name Jimbo realizes it first.

"What?" says Code Name Chase William.

"How many?" Code Name Jimbo asks.

"I count six."

"That many?" Jimbo wonders.

"Six what?" Code Name Chase William is going nuts.

Six bicycles.

Two Kissy Kitty bicycles.

Two Magical Baby Katie bicycles.

Two Bitsy Ballerina Beauty Rides.

"Don't you see?" I say to him. "Six bicycles! Six pink bicycles!"

Chapter Eight

The Freaky Joe Club Has a Narrow Escape

"So what? So there are six pink bicycles. Actually there are seven, counting mine," Secret Agent Code Name Chase William corrects me. "So big deal."

"The big deal is, I count six boys in the pool," I point out.

54

"Six boys who seem to have borrowed bicycles to get here," Code Name Jimbo adds.

"You guys are nuts," Code Name Chase William claims. "I might even say you are getting a little freaky." He gives one of those noiseless, wide-mouthed, shoulder-shaking laughs. The kind a person gives when he thinks he has been pretty funny. The annoying kind.

"There's only one way to find out. We have to conduct an investigation. Which," I explain, "is what members of a secret crime-fighting club do. Before we go into the pool, we should write down all the clues from our patrol. Freaky Joe Rule Number Three: Always Remember Your Clues."

I pull out my handy dandy, small, clue-writing notebook from my back pocket.

55

"I already wrote them down," Code Name Chase William says. A bit smugly.

"How?" I wonder.

"I found a notebook in her unicorn's secret pouch. Only I don't see how a secret pouch that anyone who watches television can find out about is so very secret." He hands me a pink piece of a Bitty Bunny sticker book.

"I wrote mine down as well," Code Name Jimbo adds. After much patting of all his clothing, he produces a candy wrapper. "I unfolded it, and wrote down what I saw so I wouldn't forget."

I take the well-used candy wrapper, holding it by one tiny corner.

"Don't worry, it's not gross," Code Name Jimbo reassures me. "I licked it clean before I wrote on it."

At this moment, I think of Freaky Joe's Rule Number Twelve: A Detective Has to Be Prepared for Any Possibility. However Awful.

"Here's the plan. We check out the pool. Most importantly the people at or in the pool. We look for anyone unusual. Anything odd," I encourage my team.

Code Name Jimbo interrupts. "Maybe something as strange as a great big boy riding an itty bitty bicycle."

"Something like that," I suggest.

Then I wait till Code Name Chase William releases Code Name Jimbo from the head lock and knuckle punch he deserved. I remind myself to talk about Team Spirit at our next meeting. "The important thing is not to make a big deal about what we're doing. Not to call attention to ourselves. And remember, anyone could be the perpetrator. Don't give yourselves away."

"Anyone could be a what?" Code Name Chase William asks.

"A bad guy," I make clear.

"Got it."

"We're on the job." Code Name Jimbo is into saluting these days.

We enter the pool. We hear it.

"Marco."

Then "Polo."

And "Polo."

"Polo." Again. And again.

Questioning anyone is going to be difficult as everyone is in the pool. Playing Marco Polo. In the event that someday, someone is allowed to read these Secret Files, I will briefly explain Marco Polo.

One person is It. This person closes his eyes (or hers, if Bella, Mugsy, and the pink crowd play) and calls "Marco."

Everyone else shouts "Polo."

The one who is It tries to find the others, following the sound of their voices. Usually It has to leap high into the air, landing on his prey. It often looks like a humpback whale in full breech. Which is the word for when a humpback whale throws itself through the air. I am interested in humpback whales as well as lemurs.

We play the game a bit differently in Ship's Cove. We allow It to yell "Alligator Eyes." He can dive underwater, opening his eyes to see the player's legs. See them, not bite them, as we had to explain the kid whose mother named him Charley. Everyone else calls him Mad Dog.

If It yells "Piranha," all players have to freeze in fear for twenty seconds. A loud "Bubba Butowski" requires everyone to swim to the side of the pool and bark like a dog.

A whistle blows. "Adult Swim," the lifeguard calls.

We're in luck. Adult swim means everyone who isn't an adult must leave the pool. Supposedly this is for kids' safety, so we don't exhaust ourselves by staying in the pool all day. We know it's so the lifeguard can sit with his girlfriend for ten minutes.

As far as I can see, his girlfriend and the female lifeguard are the only girls here. Two big girls. Six little bicycles. I say we have ourselves a mystery here.

Moaning and groaning, moving at the speed of sleepy giant sea slugs, the Marco Poloers leave the pool.

"Okay, team," I whisper. "You check out the guys. I'll ask the lifeguards a few important questions. And remember: Act normal."

The lifeguard is not interested in talking to me. He is interested in showing his girlfriend how much water he can shoot into the air and onto her when he cannonballs into the pool. She shouts something loud and silly every time he does. Watching them, I'm so glad to have years before I start dating.

The other lifeguard rolls her eyes at those two, talking all the while on her cell phone. She gives me that wave that says, *I'll be with you in a minute.* It really means, *I'm on here for a while.*

The Condor's First Rule of Crime Solving: Don't Waste Time on Your First Big Case.

I rejoin my two top-notch clue-writing teammates. I wonder if my suggestion to act normal was a good one.

Code Name Chase William does a hula with one towel around his waist and another on his head. This seems to be a crowd pleaser.

Code Name Jimbo is clearly engaged in a contest to see who can throw a cheese puff the highest and catch it in his mouth. This is an easy contest to call. He is so good at the cheese puff throw that we could probably get him on TV. Except for the fact that he could choke to death.

"Hey." I use the usual greeting. I get some *heys* back.

"What are you doing, Jack?" I inquire.

"A towel hula. I do the best towel hula on the planet Earth." He pauses midsway. Snaps his fingers at me. Whispers as loud as can be, "Why are you calling me Jack?"

"Could it be because your name is Jack?" Mad Dog suggests.

"Well, yes, it is. My name. But it's not always my name. Sometimes I am called . . ."

"Sometimes we call him Jackie, just to annoy him," I interrupt, giving Jack the evil eye.

Jack is confused. I leave him there. And remind myself to talk about 1) Team Spirit and 2) How Code Names Work at our next meeting. I think I will also go over 3) The Definition of *Secret*.

"Yes!" Code Name Jimbo does a little hula of his own. "Winner and still Cheese Puff Champion."

"He's good," Mad Dog admits.

"I can do that too," Jack announces.

"No, you can't," everyone answers.

"I could if I wanted," Jack declares. Cheese puff swallowers are taking the glory away from towel hula dancers. I see a good chance.

"Jack is just in a bad mood cause he had to ride here on my sister's bicycle. Her baby unicorn bicycle," I tell everyone, stretching out the word *bbbaaabbbyyy*.

"You will die later," Jack announces.

"He had no choice. Someone stole his bicycle. From right in front of my house. In broad daylight." Now we should get somewhere.

Code Name Jimbo joins the detective work. "How did you get to the pool today, M. D.?"

Mad Dog jumps up, ready for a fight. "Who told you?" he yells.

"Whoa, big fella," Code Name Jimbo backs off. "Nobody told me anything."

Mad Dog whips his towel on to the ground. "I rode a stupid Kissy Kitty bicycle. I cut my legs on her stupid Kissy Kitty claws." He shows everyone the damage.

I know about those claws. My mother and I rejected that bicycle when we were shopping for Bella's birthday bike. No claws for my sister. I wasn't for buying the baby unicorn one either. I still think any little girl or boy would be excited to have a Dragon Master of Zendra bicycle with the flaming nostrils. My mother didn't see it that way.

"This is terrible," I tell Mad Dog. Code Name Jimbo and Code Name Chase William back me up.

"Terrible."

"Terrible."

"What happened to your bicycle?"

"I don't know!" Mad Dog is still yelling. "It was in our driveway. And then it wasn't. Poof! My dad says I need to be more careful of my stuff. He's sure I left it at a friend's house."

"My bicycle is missing," Patrick, another Marco Polo guy adds. "My sitter says I must have left it at Mad Dog's."

More confessions follow. Four more missing bicycles. And one mother who said "You would lose your head if it wasn't attached to your neck." I hate that.

"Something's up!" I tell everyone. "Someone is stealing the bicycles of Ship's Cove."

"Wait till I get my hands on the guy who is doing this." Mad Dog bangs his fists together.

Jack jumps up. "I have a great idea," he declares.

Uh-oh, I think.

"Look at all of us," Jack explains. "We've all had our bikes stolen. I say let's find the guys who still have their bikes. They're the ones who probably took ours." Jack looks thrilled at his great idea.

He nods his head to the chorus of "Yeah!" and "Let's get them!" as well as "They'll be sorry!"

"Oh, Jack," I call. "Can I talk to you for a minute? Right now!"

"What?" Jack wonders. "Don't you think I have a great idea? I think I may have solved the case."

"Jack," I continue, "I need to explain something."

"How did you get to the pool?" Mad Dog asks in a suspicious voice.

"He rode his bicycle," Jack explains helpfully. "Conor and Timmy went too fast for me and I kept having to say 'slllooowww doowwwnnn.' But they didn't, noooo."

Everyone pays attention to Jack now, and he loves it. He has no idea what he's doing. Maybe I should have let him be called The Jack. A dung beetle would be more useful right now.

"So Timmy and Conor rode here on their own bicycles, huh?" Mad Dog wants to be sure.

"Oh, yeah," Jack assures him.

"What did you do with my ride?" Mad Dog asks Timmy. One inch from his face.

"Do with what?" Timmy has been catching cheese puffs instead of paying attention.

"My bicycle! You have my bicycle," Mad Dog insists.

"And mine!"

"And mine!"

"And mine!" goes the chorus, like some strange game of Marco Polo.

"What are you talking about?" Timmy asks.

"Timmy didn't take your bikes. I didn't take your bikes. We didn't take Jack's bike. In spite of the fact that he's an idiot, we've been out trying to find his bike," I say to make this clear to everyone.

"He must be in on it with you," Mad Dog decides for no reason I can see.

"Give me my bike back. I hate Kissy Kitty. It's not even a real bike." Mad Dog is living up to his name now.

"Not real."

"Not real."

"We want our bikes."

"Bikes."

"Bikes."

The voices rise.

They move toward us as a group, like some sort of strange pod people taken over by aliens.

"Bikes."

"Bikes."

"Great job, Jack," I submit as we back away from the wild-eyed mob. "Clever of you to convince them we're the bad guys."

"What are we going to do?" Timmy asks as the crowd moves forward.

"No choice," I say. "Run for it. If we get separated, meet at The Secret Place."

"Run for it?" Timmy asks. "Look how many more of them there are."

"Yeah," I cry as I turn and sprint. "But they're riding little pink bicycles. Go now."

Timmy and I jump on our bikes and ride fast.

"What about me?" Jack cries. "I'm on a Magical Baby Katie!"

"Then I suggest you break the land speed record for riding a little pink bicycle," I call over my shoulder. "'Cause you got us into this."

We ride. Fast. I hear Jack panting and yelling over my shoulder. I don't look back. For I hear other sounds. Coming closer. Calling "Death to the bicycle thieves."

Or something like that.

I don't stop for clarification.

Rule Number Two A: Detective Work Is Dangerous Business.

Chapter Nine

If You Give a Boy a Code Name

What to do? What to do? What to do? My brain turns as fast as my bicycle wheels. We cannot lead a deranged horde of pink bicycle riders to the door of The Secret Place. How can we get there without being seen?

We need breathing room.

"What . . . *gasp* . . . are we . . . *gasp* . . . going to do?" By the sound of it, Code Name Jimbo just needs breathing.

Chase William is not far behind. I can tell. The words "You guys!" sound closer.

I need help. I need an idea, fast. I need an Alien Death Ray to zap Mad Dog and his pack.

Or maybe someone who could possibly be an alien will do.

The Ship's Cove Security truck turns the corner from Ahoy Mate Boulevard. I race up.

"Mr. Butowski! Mr. Butowski!" I call out.

The Big Guy slows down. "What's wrong? Is Riley loose?" Bubba looks genuinely worried. "I took her home a few minutes ago. It was time for her nap."

"No, not Riley. But we have got a problem." I try to explain, but I am interrupted.

"You got a problem all right. A big problem." Chase William skids to a halt, leaving rubber. Pretty good considering the size of his tires.

"Are you boys still worried about that bicycle? I gotta check on Mrs. Bailey's little Napoleon. Then I'll find the fella who's goofing around," Bubba promises.

"No, no, it's not the bicycle." I explain. "There's this bunch of guys. On bicycles. They're chasing a poor little dog. Just to be mean." I put my hand over my heart to show sincerity. "Mr. Butowski, I think the doggie is scared."

I don't get to go on. Bubba leaves a trail of rubber as he screeches off.

"Impressive," Jimbo declares. "Very impressive."

"I could have thought of it," Jack insists, "if I would have thought of it."

"Freaky Joe Club Members. The danger is not yet over," I warn.

We hear a horn blast. More tire sounds.

"I'm not so sure." Jimbo listens. More loud voices. "I think Bubba might eat them."

"Let's go see that," Chase William insists.

"Let's go to The Secret Place and solve this mystery. Are we a secret crime-fighting mystery-solving club or not?" I ask.

With three bicycles in it, The Secret Place looks less empty. So does Riley, who is lying in the middle of the room looking like a 3-D dog rug. Clearly a case of Too Many Biscuits.

The Condor's Second Rule of Crime Fighting: Keep Bubba Away from Riley When We're on a Case.

Timmy appears barely able to move. He lies flat and drops crumbs of, well, something, into his mouth. Something green.

Jack circles, flapping his arms. "I cannot believe you left me. You left me there to be torn limb from limb."

"I cannot believe you suggested that Timmy and I were the Bad Guys," I point out.

"I didn't say that!"

"Did too." Timmy briefly stops eating.

"I did not." Jack leaps into the air. Landing on Timmy.

I unroll two big pieces of paper.

They roll around.

I tape the paper to the walls.

Timmy pins Jack to the floor.

I take a marker out of Riley's mouth.

Riley jumps on top of both Jack and Timmy.

I write "Important Stuff to Remember" on one piece of paper.

And then I hear noises. Riley, Jack, and Timmy lift their heads. Riley and Timmy sniff the air.

"Where are you guys? We're gonna get you guys." The sound roars back to The Secret Place from the street.

"Quiet," I order. "They'll go away."

"What if they don't?" Timmy worries. "What if we're trapped here with no food?"

"Can I help you guys?" My mom! What is she doing off the ladder?

"We're looking for Conor," Mad Dog explains. But not why.

"He's not here, sweetie." She calls all kids sweetie or some other name like sweetie. "Watch out, I'm backing up."

Where is she going?

What is she wearing?

We hold our breaths. The horde leaves.

"This is serious. Let's get to work." I pick up my marker.

Under Important Stuff to Remember I write:

1) Club members must not:

a) Suggest other club members are criminals.

b) Use a code name in front of someone who knows your real name.

c) Forget to use code names in front of strangers.

"Why?" Jack asks.

"That's the way it works," I try to explain.

"Why?" Jack asks.

"In case," Timmy answers.

"In case of what?" Jack wonders.

"Because," Timmy answers.

"I'm confused," Jack states.

"No!" Timmy says.

"Guys, we have to get this done," I insist.

Riley lifts her head slightly. Growls.

I ignore her. "I will write down all our observations. There will be a clue in there somewhere." I hope.

Riley growls again.

"Uh-oh," Timmy says. "Now it's getting ugly."

"Oh, no!" Jack says. "Not that."

The Beast is not attacking him. What can he be afraid of now?

Then I turn to the window.

And I see it.

Oh, it is a horrible sight.

Chapter Ten

Can Gorillas Swim?

I rush to the door. Fling it open. Yell with all my might.

"Shoo! Shoo!"

My sister and Mugsy press their faces to the window, noses flat and tongues out. Mugsy rotates her eyes.

"Make it stop!" Jack screams.

"Bella! Mugsy! Get lost." I say it ever so nicely.

"Can't."

"You have to watch us."

"Mom!" I yell with more than all my might.

She appears. "You have to watch them for me. Don't argue. It's an emergency."

"My brother ate a turtle," Mugsy announces.

"Conor, I'm taking Mikey to the doctor. You have to watch the girls."

My mother starts to go.

"Mom," I call.

"That's an order." She keeps going.

"You're still green," I say to her back.

"So is my brother," Mugsy adds. "Really green."

"So was the turtle," Bella adds.

The girls sit on the beanbag chairs.

I say, "Don't move."

Timmy asks, "Did he chew the turtle or swallow it whole?"

"Was it still moving?" Jack wants to know.

I write:

Seen on Patrol
JACK:

1) Manatee Maintenance for Pools truck
2) Speed's Pizza Delivery truck
3) A Very Noisy Bird
4) Gorilla Pool Service truck

TIMMY:

1) Dolphin Pool Service truck
2) Overnight Delivery Man (driving too fast)
3) Mrs. Bailey's noisy dog Napoleon on the loose
4) Dog doodoo in road (Napoleon?)
5) Gorilla Pool Service truck

CONOR:

1) Bubba and Riley in the truck

2) Lucky Larry's Home Grooming
   Service truck

3) Gorilla Pool Service truck

4) Special Squid Service for Pools
   truck

5) Overnight Delivery Man (Driving
   too fast. Tell Mom.)

"No fair," Jack complains. "You both have more than me."

"But you had the most important clue," Timmy replies. "I mean, that noisy bird is going to crack the case."

"It was a Very Noisy Bird," Jack corrects him.

"I heard a noisy bird once," Bella states.

"My brother ate a noisy bird once," Mugsy adds.

"Jack has one in his brain," Timmy whispers.

"I heard that." Jack starts to move.

"We must follow Rule Number Twelve A. Right now!" I shout over the girls' imitations of noisy birds. "Analyze Your Clues. The Answer Is There. So let's go over the list."

"The pizza man would never be a bad guy," Timmy insists. We all agree.

I cross him off. And the bird. And Napoleon. And any stuff that might have come from Napoleon.

"The overnight delivery man drives too fast," I suggest. "He wouldn't have time to steal." Everyone agrees. He's gone.

"I don't think Bubba has time," Jack says. "He's too busy." Yup. Bubba leaves the list of suspects. "And that Lucky Larry guy has a whole store in his truck. Where would he put the bikes?" Larry joins Bubba.

"Okay. Here are our suspects: Special Squid

Service, Manatee Maintenance, The Dolphin Man, and Gorilla Pool Service. Can we eliminate any of them?" I ask. "Did we notice anything unusual that we should talk about? Any big clues?"

Big "nopes" from everyone, including Bella and Mugsy.

"But I did have a thought this morning," Timmy says. "I need to look at *Animals of the World.* I'll look up *gorillas.*"

"I'll investigate Squid Service," I say. "Jack, pick one of the others and get to work."

I grab *The Big Book of Undersea Life.* Look up *squid.* Write down useful facts about squids. Then I take the word and hold it up to the mirror. Nothing there. I try rearranging the letters. I end up with *quisd, sdqui,* and *idqus.* I decide *idqus* has possibility. It might be a lost tribe of the Incan civilization. I decide to check the encyclopedia.

"I was right!" Timmy interrupts my train of thought. I look up and see him and Riley sharing a biscuit. Jack and the girls are lying on their stomachs, moving their arms and legs in a strange way.

"Jack, how is that helping?" I want to know.

"I'm teaching them the dolphin kick," he explains. "It helps me to get inside the mind of the master criminal." Bella and Mugsy give high-pitched dolphin shrieks.

"Only if it's the Dolphin guy. I'm pretty sure I am on to something with squid."

Timmy slams the book shut. "I am right, I am right!" he announces again. "Gorillas do not live in water."

"Of course they don't. They live in the highlands of Central Africa." He only had to ask me.

"Exactly!" Timmy holds the book over his head and does that weird end-zone dance again.

Jack bends his knees, drops his arms, and

makes loud, strange, junglelike noises. Bella and Mugsy do too. This is all so helpful.

Timmy points at the list. "Dolphin—Water. Manatee—Water. Squid—Water. Gorilla—no water." He looks so proud. "Get it?"

"Not really." I am itching to get to the encyclopedia.

"It's a clue," Timmy insists. "And his truck is the only one seen by all three of us. And I have never seen Gorilla Pool Service before. Have you?"

"Nope," Jack declares.

"Nope, nope," Bella and Mugsy have no idea, but they chime in.

I give in. "Okay, I haven't seen him before. It's a clue. Very good observation, Code Name Jimbo. The Gorilla Pool Service has done a poor job of choosing their name."

Jack stops beating his chest for a minute. "They chose bad uniforms, too," he adds. "That mask has got to be hot."

Bella and Mugsy still stomp and hoot.

Jimbo looks at me. "You have a strange look on your face."

I move slowly toward Jack. I ask, "Mask?"

"Yeah, the mask." Jack explains. "Hello? The one the driver was wearing. The Gorilla mask. Duh?"

Chapter Eleven

Everyone Loves a Parade

"Let me get this straight, Jack. You saw the driver of the Gorilla Pool Service company? And he was wearing a gorilla mask? So no one could see his face?"

"That would be a big yes!" Jack answers proudly. "Guess I observed better than you."

"And when I asked if you noticed anything unusual, wouldn't that leap to the front of your brain? Wearing a hot gorilla mask while driving around a neighborhood? To clean pools?"

"I guess not," Jack replies. "Hey girls, want to play manatee?"

What came over me? I cannot say. I only know this. One minute Jack was on the ground being a manatee. The next minute I was flying through the air. I looked exactly like Bobby Orr scoring the most amazing goal in the history of hockey.

That picture should go on the wall of The Secret Place.

I land on Jack. I actually wrestle. Riley joins in. Timmy, Bella, and Mugsy make a line. Dancing. Singing. "Go, Conor. Go, Conor. Go, Conor."

As I say, I do not know what came over me.

So, here we are again. On patrol. Only now we know what we're looking for. Only we don't look like a patrol. We look like a parade.

On my bike, I pull Bella in a purple wagon.

Timmy pulls Mugsy in a pink one. The girls are both holding magic wands. Which they looked for while we lost precious time.

Jack rides the baby unicorn bike while holding on to Riley's leash. Riley keeps speeding up. Which tips Jack over. Which makes him whine some more about having to hold the leash of a man-eating beast.

"Do we have a plan?" Timmy wants to know.

"We're looking for the Gorilla Man," I explain.

"And then what?"

"When we find him, we'll make a plan," I promise.

"Shouldn't we have a plan now?" Jack asks, getting back on Baby Katie. Again.

"Mad Dog has a plan now," Timmy points out. "He plans to hurt us."

I don't answer. Every time I try to speak, the

words Gorilla Mask bang around in my brain.

Bella and Mugsy sing a little ditty they make up as they go along.

"Mad Dog Mad Dog, he ate a turtle,
He kissed a noisy bird
which made the bird go . . ."

"I see him!" Jimbo shouts. "He turned into Mrs. Bailey's street."

Now I have a plan. "Jack, take my bicycle. Ride as fast as you can to Mrs. Bailey's house."

"I'm there." Jack leaps to action. Leaps to the bigger machine.

"Listen carefully, Jack. Mrs. Bailey will be at work. Napoleon is riding around with Bubba. You leave the bicycle on the front lawn. Then hide in the bushes. Really hide. Not pretend to hide," I instruct. "Got it?"

"I got it." Jack flies off.

"He's going to hide the bicycle in the bushes," Timmy says. "And lie down on the front lawn."

"He might," I admit.

"Why is Timmy so wobbly?" Bella wants to know.

Timmy pulls a wagon and holds on to Riley. I balance on the unicorn, tugging Mugsy. Freaky Joe had no suggestions or rules to cover this situation.

"Why did you send Jack?"

"Because he can break the land-speed record. Because there'd be no one to help me with the Gorilla Man if you two are rolling around on the ground," I explain.

"Good point," Timmy agrees. "Except who was the last person to roll around on the ground? Come on, girls." We ride into danger to the sound of "Go, Conor. Go, Conor. Go, Conor."

"Sssshhhh!" I hissed loudly.

The Gorilla Man drives slowly up The Lime in

the Coconut Lane. There is a bicycle, not a boy, on Mrs. Bailey's lawn.

"This is it! We are about to solve our first case," I announce. "This is great."

"Now what?" Timmy asks.

"We leave the girls, the bicycles, the wagons, and the magic wands here," I explain.

"And?"

"When he goes to get the bike, we get him." So simple.

"Get him?" Tim asks.

"Yeah, we get him. You girls sit here and don't move. Or you know what."

"Get him?" Tim repeats himself.

"Yes, get him." This is not hard.

"How?"

"The way detectives get bad guys." I have to do everything.

"How?" is the next question.

"Quiet. He's almost to the house. He is slowing. Slowing," I observe.

"Passing. He is passing." Timmy uses a sportscaster's voice. "And the Gorilla Man does not stop to steal a bike."

"Aaaarrrgggghhhhh," is my answer.

"I think Mad Dog sees us," is his reply.

Chapter Twelve

Green Momma Time

"So what now?" Timmy wants to know.

"What is 'you know what'?" Bella asks.

"What?" Mugsy asks.

Jack stands on the lawn, his arms wide, yelling, "What?"

"Let's go," I say.

"And what?" everyone asks.

"Not get him," I sigh.

"Why didn't he stop? Why didn't he take the bike? He couldn't see me, I promise. I was hidden. Over there." Jack is breaking the land-speed record for talking. "What do we do now?"

"Not get him," Timmy helps out.

"We go back to The Secret Place. We start

over." I guess I'll look up the lost tribe of *Idqus.* Maybe they were famed for stealing wheels.

"I say we panic," Timmy suggests.

"Or ride very very fast," Jack agrees. "We'll have to leave the girls."

Mad Dog and his Merry Marco Poloers are riding in our general direction. They are not quite in the street. Yet.

"They haven't seen us. Let's go."

"No," I insist. "Everyone hide. Quickly. Leave everything here."

The Gorilla Man has stopped. And is turning. Maybe he hasn't seen us.

"To the trees!" I call. We all run. We all hide.

Then the Gorilla Man stops right in front of Mrs. Bailey's house. And gets out of the truck. And picks up Magic Baby Katie the unicorn.

"My bike," Bella whispers.

I put my hand over her mouth. "Don't say anything." She licks my palm. Completely disgusting.

Even Riley is quiet as Timmy feeds him something I do not want to know.

Then Mad Dog and his merry men arrive at one end of the street. "I swear I saw them here," one boy yells.

Then the blue-and-purple truck of Bubba Butowski, Ace Security Man, pulls into the street to bring Napoleon home.

The Gorilla Man puts down the bicycle when he sees Mad Dog's horde.

The horde freezes when they see Bubba.

Bubba leaps from his truck when he sees them. Well, gets out. Bubba does not leap. He is a big man.

"Now!" I yell.

"Now we get him?" Timmy asks.

The Freaky Joe Club charges down the lawn. Bella and Mugsy give the dolphin call.

Everyone comes together at the Gorilla Man's truck.

Bubba speaks first.

"Hey, Riley. Hello, the Big R. Who's a good girl?"

"What in the name of blue blazes are y'all doing?" the Gorilla Man demands to know.

Mad Dog says, "You guys are goners." Or something like that.

"Bubba," I tell him, "you have to arrest this man."

"What?" says the Gorilla Man.

"What?" says Mad Dog.

"Now boys, stop playing," Bubba insists.

"He's the thief," I shout. "The bicycle thief!"

"Look," the Gorilla Man says to Bubba, "I'm working on a job. I'm driving through the neighborhood. I see this cute little bike lying in the street, so I stop to move it. And then I see these nutcases come running at me."

"I like nuts," Bella says.

"My brother eats nuts," Mugsy adds.

"Don't worry. It's just kids being kids," Bubba advises Gorilla Man. "Say, do you have a dog? I have some great treats in my truck."

"Mr. Butowski!" I shout.

"I gotta drive," says the Gorilla. "I'm late."

Then my mother arrives in her truck. Not looking happy. Still green. She gets out with Mugsy's little brother. "What are you boys doing here?"

"Mom," I call. "You have to help."

"Mrs. M., the boys are being goofy and bothering this nice man while he works," Bubba begins to explain.

"Why is that nice man wearing a gorilla mask?" my mother wants to know.

"I gotta drive," the Gorilla Man says again. He starts to get in his truck.

"Timmy, let loose The Beast." I go to Plan L.

The Beast is happy to be loose. She runs to her buddy Bubba. She runs to annoy Jack. She runs over to the Gorilla Man's truck. Riley knows what people keep in their trucks. She jumps up to say hello and get her share.

"Get out of here, you stupid mutt." The Gorilla Man gives Riley a kick.

"Hey!" shouts my mother. But her words are drowned out.

By the Great Noise coming from Bubba's mouth.

"YOU KICKED A DOG! WHAT KIND OF MAN WOULD KICK A DOG?" The Big Man is in fast motion. What a sight to say I saw.

"Aw, get lost," the Gorilla Man says. "You are all a bunch of nuts."

"DON'T YOU EVER KICK A DOG IN BUBBA'S NEIGHBORHOOD!" With each word, Bubba bangs the side of the truck hard.

Bubba is a big guy. His banging shakes the truck. Which causes the back door to pop open. Which shows everyone a truck full of bicycles.

"My bike!" Jack shouts.

"Not that again," Timmy moans.

"Bubba. Bubba! It's the missing bicycles," I shout.

"This man is a thief," my mother realizes. "Stop him."

Bubba stops. To pick up Riley. "Poor girl. Poor poor baby."

The Gorilla Man bolts. Runs. Is getting away.

"Get him!" I yell.

"Now we get him?" Timmy asks.

"My bike," says Jack.

Mad Dog, everyone else is in the truck.

"Oh, man," I cry. "He's getting away."

But I forgot about Mom.

The Green Lady runs fast too. She almost has him. She takes a flying leap. And brings him down.

Timmy and I run up. We help the Amazing Mom sit on the Gorilla Man.

Mugsy's brother Mikey runs up. Looks at the Gorilla Man. "Do you want to see my turtle?" he asks.

"Go, Momma. Go, Momma. Go, Momma," Bella and Mugsy chant.

Bubba arrives carrying Riley over his shoulder. He picks up the Gorilla Man with his other arm.

My mom calls the police.

Everyone gets his bicycle back.

Everyone looks at Mikey's turtle.

"I didn't swallow him. I licked him, but he tasted bad. So I put him in my pants," Mikey explains.

The Gorilla Man goes away in a police car.

Riley goes away in Bubba's truck.

"I'll keep her for a while," he says. "Help her get over the shock." Riley leans her head on the window. She looks sad. What an act.

Mom goes away with Mikey, Mugsy, Bella, two wagons, seven pink bicycles, and one turtle. The Marco Poloers are going to follow her as she delivers the bikes. My mother is now completely cool. If still green.

"We'll be home soon," I promise my mother.

"Well done, Conor," she says.

"You were pretty awesome yourself," I answer.

"But you figured it out," she reminds me.

"We all did," I tell her the truth. "I just organized us."

"I expect nothing less from The Condor," she says, pulling away.

I turn to the other two. There can be only three.

"WWWHHHOOOOOOOO!" I shout. We high five.

Timmy does that end-zone dance thing. Jack does the same. He adds some finger snapping.

I join in. Freaky Joe would be so proud of us. The Freaky Joe Club lives again!

And so that is how it was on the first day. On our first case.

It turns out Bubba Butowski got the credit for solving the case. The neighborhood gave him a thank-you present. The local paper wrote a small story.

"I couldn't have done this without help," Bubba was quoted as saying. "That great dog Riley Moloney is the one who showed me the way." There was a picture of Riley and Bubba.

Ah, well. We of the Freaky Joe Club know the truth. And I have written it down here in the book. So one day the truth may be known.

I close the book, lock the bicycle lock. Our secrets are safe for now. Lie back in the baseball

LATE EDITION EXTRA

LOCAL SECURITY GUARD BREAKS UP BICYCLE THEFT RING

chair. Pick up *The Adventures of Remington Reedmarsh, Lemur Detective, Volume 10.*

There is nothing like a good mystery book. Reading one makes any day a good day.

Want to Have Another Good Day?
Coming Soon from the Freaky Joe Club

Secret File #2:
The Case of the Smiling Shark